Billy Tibbles Moves Out!

↑ Tom (Dad) ~ says he's permanently harassed. Not very good with cameras.

Valentina (that's Mum)→ Likes a peaceful house and high-heeled fluffy mules. Total glamourpuss.

(a big purry thank you to Sue and Sally)

Billy: being silly, as usual. Likes skateboards and teasing Twinkle.

↑ Little Baby Eric. Wise beyond his years. Likes purple blankets.

For Shelley and Mark

First published in Great Britain by HarperCollins Publishers Ltd in 2003

1 3 5 7 9 10 8 6 4 2

ISBN: 0-00-714333-8

Text/illustrations copyright © Jan Fearnley 2003

The author/illustrator asserts the moral right to be identified as the author/illustrator of the work.

The HarperCollins website address is: www.fireandwater.com

Printed and bound in China

Twinkle ---→ Trainee glamourpuss. Likes glittery things and teasing Billy. (Secretly covets the high-heeled fluffy mules)

Billy Tibbles' bedroom was his favourite place.

Sometimes it was tidy.

Mostly it was messy.

Billy liked mess.

Billy's sister, Twinkle, had her own room, too. Billy wasn't allowed in there…

…but he didn't care.
Billy liked his room best.
He had his toys
and his books…

...and his skateboard
(which he wasn't
supposed to ride in
the house)...

...and his squeaky, creaky bed.
And best of all, Billy had it
all to himself.

"Now then, Dad," said Billy, wagging a cheeky finger, "remember, everybody shares in our house – AND THAT MEANS YOU, TOO!"

So Dad moved over to
make room, because
Dads have to share,
just like everyone else.
  The children leapt
aboard the big, cosy
bed and, eventually,
everybody had a very
good night's sleep.

Well, almost everybody.